The Little Blue Dog

By
Karen J Roberts

ISBN: 1469907194
ISBN-13: 9781469907192

Library of Congress Control Number: 2012900792
CreateSpace, North Charleston, SC

Dedicated to my mom and dad.

Adopt! Don't Shop!

Karen
&
Louie 🐾

One sunny afternoon in California, a tiny puppy was born. He was called a "designer dog" which is a fancy way of saying he was a mutt. The puppy was very cute, just like all puppies are. His daddy was a Chihuahua, and his mommy was an Italian Greyhound.

The tiny puppy had smooth blue colored fur with white paws and a white chest. He was very soft and snuggly. He sat in the window of a puppy store in a shopping mall with a lot of other very cute little designer dogs. One day a nice girl picked him out of all the other little puppies in the store. She took him to his new home and became his new owner. He learned to walk on a leash, go potty outside, and have very nice manners. He was such a good boy and he was happy.

The tiny puppy grew into a handsome little blue dog.
But then one day he noticed all these card board boxes in
his house. His owner was putting all of her things in
the boxes and the house was becoming very
empty. Soon she put his toys and his food
bowl in a box too. The little blue dog
started to feel very nervous.

The next day his owner took him for a ride in the car. He usually loved going for car rides, but something was different this time. She was very sad, and that made him sad too. She took him into a strange place he had never been before. She was crying as she handed the little blue dog over to the strange woman saying she just couldn't keep him anymore.

The next thing he knew, he was in a cage all by himself. He could hear lots of other dogs barking and crying. He was trying to be brave, but he was sad and lonely and scared. He didn't know why he was in this cage, but he wanted to go home.

There were nice people who would bring him food and water. A few times a day they would take him for a walk. He got to see all the other little dogs that were also there in cages. They were all cute and little, just like him. But they were also scared and wanted to go home.

After fourteen scary and lonely days of living in the cage, he and a group of the other little dogs were all taken to the airport. The little blue dog had never seen an airport, and he had never been on an airplane. All the little dogs were very brave even though they did not know where they were going. They did their best to behave on the long flight.

After many hours on the plane they arrived in Boston, Massachusetts. The little blue dog thought maybe he was finally going home. But when he ended up in another cage at a different place, he was beginning to lose hope. He wasn't sure how his life had become so uncertain. He just wanted to go home.

The people at this new place were very nice to him, but he was still very scared and lonely. All day strange new people would walk by and look at him and talk to him. Sometimes he would get to play in a small room with one of these strangers before being put back in the cage.

The little blue dog spent twelve more lonely days and nights in this new cage wondering what he had to done to end up without a home.

Just when he was about to give up hope, a very nice woman knelt down in front of his cage. She was kind and gentle. He got up the nerve to walk over to her so she could reach her fingers through the cage. He sniffed her hand and she gently scratched him under the chin.

"Hello little blue dog" she said in a soft voice.

The little blue dog wagged his tail, put his ears back and sighed.

After spending some time in the small room with the nice woman, something miraculous happened. She didn't put him back in his cage. Instead, she hugged him with joy, kissed his face, and said "I'll take him!"

She carried the little blue dog out to her car.
He was still a little nervous because he had
such a difficult time the past four weeks
and he wasn't sure where he was going.
But the nice woman hugged him and made
him feel safe.

Finally he arrived and saw his new home. There was a very nice yard with soft green grass, and that made his tail wag. The nice woman said "Your new name is Louie. I am your new mommy and this is your new home. You will never have to spend another night in a cage again." This made his tail wag even more. He was very happy to have a new home, but he was even happier to meet his new family.

The little blue dog now named "Louie" had two new brothers. His brother Jackson was a Chihuahua and he looked a lot like Louie. His other brother Mackie was a red and white Cavalier Spaniel. They were both very nice to him and made him feel welcome. They showed him his new yard and shared their toys with him. He was so happy to have brothers to play with!

He followed Mackie and Jackson around the house to the backyard. Boy was Louie surprised when he met the twelve hens who lived in a big chicken coop. They were very pretty and didn't mind dogs. The hens came over to him clucking and cooing and they made Louie feel very welcome.

When he went inside his new home for the first time, he met his two new sisters, who were both cats. They were bigger than him and very fluffy. Mia and Squeeky were curled up sleeping peacefully in the sun. Looking at them made him feel warm and safe, and he could hear them purring as he walked by.

When his new mommy showed him his very own soft and cozy bed on the couch, he happily leaped into it. She covered him up with a soft blanket and kissed him on his head and said "Welcome home Louie, we love you."

The little blue dog now named Louie felt happy and loved. For the first time in long time, he wasn't scared. He drifted off to sleep, dreaming of his new life that would be filled with long walks in the park, games of chase and race with his brothers and a warm bed at night. Life was good again. He said a prayer for all the other little dogs who were still living in the scary cages, hoping they would soon find a safe and loving new place to call home.

The End

Photo Credit: Peter Meo

To learn more about Louie and Karen,
visit
www.thelittlebluedog.com